RAVEN

Titles in Teen Reads:

New Dawn DANIEL BLYTHE	**Raven** TOMMY DONBAVAND	**Remember Rosie** BEVERLY SANFORD
Underworld SIMON CHESHIRE	**Ward 13** TOMMY DONBAVAND	**The Wishing Doll** BEVERLY SANFORD
Dawn of the Daves TIM COLLINS	**Fair Game** ALAN DURANT	**Billy Button** CAVAN SCOTT
Joke Shop TIM COLLINS	**By My Side** ANN EVANS	**Mama Barkfingers** CAVAN SCOTT
Mr Perfect TIM COLLINS	**Nightmare** ANN EVANS	**Pest Control** CAVAN SCOTT
The Locals TIM COLLINS	**Insectoids** ROGER HURN	**The Changeling** CAVAN SCOTT
Troll TIM COLLINS	**Jigsaw Lady** TONY LEE	**The Hunted** CAVAN SCOTT
Copy Cat TOMMY DONBAVAND	**Mister Scratch** TONY LEE	**Sitting Target** JOHN TOWNSEND
Dead Scared TOMMY DONBAVAND	**Noticed** TONY LEE	**Deadly Mission** MARK WRIGHT
Just Bite TOMMY DONBAVAND	**Stalker** TONY LEE	**Ghost Bell** MARK WRIGHT
Home TOMMY DONBAVAND	**Death Road** JON MAYHEW	**The Corridor** MARK WRIGHT
Kidnap TOMMY DONBAVAND	**Snow White, Black Heart** JACQUELINE RAYNER	**World Without Words** JONNY ZUCKER

Badger Publishing Limited, Oldmedow Road, Hardwick Industrial Estate, King's Lynn PE30 4JJ
Telephone: 01438 791037

www.badgerlearning.co.uk

RAVEN

TOMMY DONBAVAND

Raven ISBN 978-1-78464-329-4

Publisher: Susan Ross
Senior Editor: Danny Pearson
Editorial Coordinator: Claire Morgan
Copyeditor: Cheryl Lanyon
Designer: Bigtop Design Ltd
Printed by Bell and Bain Ltd, Glasgow

2 4 6 8 10 9 7 5 3 1

CHAPTER 1

SNAKE

I tiptoed down the stairs, then took a moment to calm my breath before I went into the living room. This wasn't going to go well — I already knew that — so I might as well be ready for the row that was about to come.

I took a last moment to enjoy the peace and quiet, then I went inside.

Mum was sitting in her chair, sipping tea and reading the paper while some classical music nonsense played on the radio. There was no sign of Dad, which meant he was probably out in the shed, working on one of his wooden models.

My parents are so sensible they make me want to scream!

I slumped onto the couch, grabbed the remote and turned on the TV. It didn't matter which channel I picked, I would only get to watch a few seconds before my mum looked up…

She actually spat out a mouthful of tea!

"Poppy!" she cried.

"Raven," I corrected. "People call me Raven now."

"Not under my roof they don't!" Mum snapped. "What in the name of all that is holy have you done to your hair?"

I jumped up and examined my new shocking-pink tresses in the mirror. "Don't you like it?" I teased.

"Like it?" Mum bellowed. "I forbade it! I specifically said you were NOT to dye your hair."

"No, you didn't," I said as calmly as I could. "You said I couldn't dye my hair jet black. You didn't say anything at all about Hollywood Candy!"

"Hollywood what?"

"That's the name of the hair dye I used."

"Well, whatever it's called, you can go and wash it out right now!"

"Can't," I pointed out. "It's permanent."

"What!"

"Yep," I smiled. "So, I guess the only way to make it look more – ooh, I dunno – sensible, would be to dye it again, but a darker colour this time."

"You are not having black hair, young lady!"

"Then I guess we're stuck with pink…"

Mum practically growled deep in her throat. "Just wait until your father hears about this…"

"He already has," I said. "He's only at the bottom of the garden, and you're making enough noise to be heard streets away. It's no wonder Stephen ran away – he couldn't stand listening to you any more."

That was it; I'd gone too far, and I knew it. Mum leaped out of her chair and slapped my face. Hard. I felt my skin redden and burn, but I wasn't going to cry. I wasn't going to let her win.

"Don't you dare bring your brother into this," she snarled, fighting back her own tears. "This has nothing to do with him."

"Of course it does!" I said. "Everything has to do with Stephen these days. Ever since he vanished, you won't let me go out at night, you won't let me stay over at my friends' houses, nothing! You keep me in here like a prisoner!"

"It's for your own good!" Mum replied through gritted teeth. She snatched up the newspaper and stabbed a finger at the article she had been reading. "Those weird people were seen in the woods again last night – messing around. Some people say it's black magic. Satanic rituals. That's what could happen to you!"

I shook my head in disbelief. "What? I'm going to strip naked and dance for the devil just because I've dyed my hair?"

"That's how these things start, Poppy!"

"Only in your head!" I turned away from her and focused on the single light burning in the shed at the far end of the garden. Dad spent almost all of his time down there these days, working on his models.

"You have to let me have a life, Mum," I said. "You have to stop smothering me. I'm not Stephen, OK? I'm not going to disappear just because you let me hang around with my friends after dark once in a while."

I heard Mum sit back in her chair and the rustle of the newspaper as she tossed it aside. Then she turned the volume on the radio up; she didn't want me to hear her crying.

Without looking round, I left the living room and hurried back upstairs. Once inside my bedroom, I grabbed a baby mouse from the box and dropped it into the glass tank to give Tonto, my pet snake, his dinner. Then I lay back on my bed, trying not to listen to the classical music echoing softly from downstairs.

I hadn't meant to upset Mum. I never did. I just wish she'd listen to me sometimes. But, since Stephen had upped and left in the middle of the night, she wouldn't let me do a thing.

If only there was a way I could talk to Stephen. To ask him to at least ring Mum and say he was OK. Maybe that way we'd all be able to stop worrying and get on with our lives. But, after seven months without so much as a postcard, that wasn't going to be easy. Or was it…?

I reached under my pillow to slide out a leather-bound book and flicked through its delicately handwritten pages. Across the room, there were a few squeaks as Tonto tucked into his evening meal – then, silence.

I began to read.

CHAPTER 2

COW

"Are you nuts?" exclaimed Angel near the end of double maths the next morning. "You're going to go through with it?"

I shrugged. "I think so," I said. "Why not?"

"Because it's witchcraft!"

"Shut up!" I hissed. "Are you trying to get me into trouble again?"

I'd only just got back to class following a half-hour lecture about the 'inappropriate colour of my hair' by Miss Cowl, the deputy head (or Miss Cow, as everyone called her).

Apparently, it 'didn't give out a positive image of the school', and I had three days to return my hair to its usual, dull chestnut-brown.

"But this is serious, Poppy…"

"Raven!"

"OK, Raven, whatever! You still shouldn't be mucking around with that stuff."

"Relax, I know what I'm doing…"

Angel shook her head. "No, you don't," she said flatly. "That's why you had to buy that weird book off the internet."

"So?"

"So – you had it delivered to my house, without telling me! What if my dad had seen it?"

"He didn't, did he?"

No, but he might have – and he's the church choir master!"

I sighed. It was easy for Angel. Her family had allowed her to dye her hair black, and hadn't complained when she had dropped the final letter 'a' from the end of her name. They even signed forms to say that the teachers should call her by her new name at school.

The bell rang and we set off towards our next lesson – chemistry. Kids in the corridors pointed at my hair as we passed, and some even laughed. I didn't mind, though. It was better than being pointed at because I was the girl with the missing twin brother.

We picked two seats near the back of the chemistry lab and dumped our bags under the desk.

"So, what do you have to do?" asked Angel. "Summon up a demon, or something?"

"Don't be stupid!" I said. "I'm just trying to find Stephen, not damn him to all eternity in the fires of Hell."

Angel's eyes widened. "Does the book tell you how to do that?" she gasped.

"Oh yeah," I said, trying to keep a straight face. "You can damn people to Hell, have them eaten by hungry imps, or even curse someone so that their toenails become too hard to cut with normal scissors."

I watched as Angel shook her head in disbelief. "That's disgusting!"

"No," I began, "I didn't really mean— " But I didn't get any further because, at that moment, Tiffany Langer and her little gang strode into the classroom looking as though they owned it.

I groaned. They were coming our way – although I don't know how they walked anywhere without falling flat on their faces because they had their eyes fixed down on the screens of their mobile phones the whole time.

Tiffany stopped beside where I was sitting and struck a pose. Her friends placed themselves around their leader as though she was royalty, and not just the most popular girl in school. Like all her gang, Tiffany had adapted her school uniform in such a way that she looked like a dancer in a rap video.

"Like, you're in our seats," she said, without looking up from her phone.

I glanced at Angel and back again. "I'm sorry?"

"These seats," Tiffany explained. "They're, like, ours…"

I shrugged. "I can't see your name on them anywhere…"

Eventually, Tiffany finished tapping her phone with long, pink nails and hit Send. There was a flurry of buzzes as her gang's phones all vibrated at once, and then they all giggled together.

I laughed, too. "Oh, my God!" I said. "Are you lot texting each other?"

Tiffany's eyes flickered away from her screen for a moment and she looked me up and down from beneath her false eyelashes. "So, like, what's it got to do with you, yeah?" she demanded.

"She didn't!" blurted out one of her gang.

"Whatever!" exclaimed another.

I looked from face to face – each covered with the same, slightly orange make-up, and each head topped with an identical pineapple-sized bun of streaked hair.

"It doesn't matter," I said with a glance towards Angel. "You wouldn't get the irony."

Tiffany glared at me. "Are you sayin' I'm stupid, yeah?" I felt her gang step closer in.

"She didn't!"

"Whatever!"

"I didn't say anything," I promised.

"Yeah, well…" Tiffany clicked her chewing gum and started on another text. "You'd better not go sayin' I'm stupid or nuffink. I ain't taking that grief from some dirty goth girl!"

Before I knew it, I was on my feet and staring into her eyes. "What did you just call me?"

Tiffany continued to chomp on her gum with an open mouth for a minute. "I know you," she said.

I didn't move. "Oh, you do – do you?"

Tiffany nodded. "Yeah. You're that Poppy sumfink, innit!"

"My name is Raven."

Tiffany sniffed. "Whatever. You're still that girl with the dead brother."

I felt Angel rest a hand on my shoulder, but I pushed it away. "Stephen isn't dead," I growled.

"Shame," said Tiffany, still staring at her phone screen. "It would be one less dirty goth in the world if he was."

I found out later I'd broken her nose with the first punch.

CHAPTER 3

BAT

"Suspended!" Mum shouted, for about the fifth time in two minutes.

I settled back in my seat and watched the traffic pass by the window. "Just for a week," I reminded her.

"I don't care how long it's for!" Mum yelled, pulling out onto the main road. "No one in our family has ever been suspended before."

I sighed. It was bad enough that she'd been called out of work to come and pick me up from school, but now I was letting the good name of the family down.

"Your father will have something to say about this!"

"No, he won't," I said flatly. "He'll just go and hide in the shed again."

We drove for a few miles in an awkward silence. When Mum spoke again, her voice was quieter, but no less angry.

"Don't you think I have it hard enough already, Poppy?" she asked.

"Raven," I corrected.

"Poppy!" she insisted. "I've tried to protect you, I really have. But you just seem to want to do things to hurt me all the time."

"It's not like that," I promised her. "I know you're trying to protect me – and I'm grateful, I really am. But, it's too much. You even freaked out when I asked if I could dye my hair black."

"Your brother dyed his hair black, and look what happened!"

I stared at her for a second, my mouth opening and closing. "Wha—? You can't…" I almost screamed with frustration. "He didn't run away because of the colour of his hair, Mum!"

She spun to face me, her eyes red. "Then why did he go?"

"I… I don't know. None of us do. The police said some kids just go missing. Most of them come home when they're ready to talk about whatever's— "

Suddenly, Mum slammed on the brakes and brought the car to an emergency stop in the middle of the road. I heard screeching tyres behind us, then angry shouting and several car horns.

"What is it?" I asked her. "What's wrong?"

But Mum wasn't looking at me any more, she was staring over my shoulder and out of the car window. "Stephen?" she croaked.

Whipping off her seatbelt, she flung the car door open and raced across the other lane of traffic, narrowly avoiding being hit by a bus, as she chased after a tall figure in a grey hoodie. He had jet-black hair.

"Mum!" I yelled, leaping out of my own seat and running after her. Horns blared as cars skidded to a halt. I mouthed *Sorry*! to a very angry couple, then reached the pavement and looked around.

I'd lost them!

Scanning the crowds of shoppers, I fought to get my breath back under control. Then I heard a shout from the direction of the shopping mall, and caught a glimpse of Mum as she pushed past a woman in a wheelchair and disappeared inside. I set off running again.

Could she really have seen Stephen? After all these months, is that how we would discover what had happened? Just catching a glimpse of him in the street?

I rounded the corner of the bakery and raced into the covered mall. There were fewer people in here, but the polished floor made it difficult to gain as much ground and, within a few seconds, I'd lost sight of Mum again.

I started ducking into shop doorways and jumping up to try to see over the heads of the shoppers. The newsagent's, the shoe shop, the optician's. Mum wasn't in any of them.

I reached into my pocket for my mobile phone. If I was lucky, Mum might just have had hers with her when she—

My pocket was empty. I must have lost my phone somewhere between jumping out of the car into moving traffic and dashing into the building. That was all I needed.

I turned, resigned to heading back to the car and waiting for Mum to return. And that's when I heard the shout: "Get off me, you mad old bat!"

And the cry that followed: "But, Stephen… it's me!"

I followed the sound of the argument as it escalated and found Mum in the doorway of a coffee shop, trying to hug some random guy. He was the figure with the dyed-black hair and the grey hoodie. The one Mum had chased through town.

"Mum," I said, quietly, "that's not Stephen…"

She looked at me, her eyes almost begging me not to say those words. "It is Stephen," she whispered hoarsely. "It has to be!"

I took her hand, pulling her away from the furious stranger. "I'm sorry, Mum," I croaked. "It looks like him, but it's not."

"Is she with you?" the guy demanded.

I nodded, wiping my tears on the sleeve of my school blazer. "She thought you were someone else."

"Yeah, well – you want to keep her under control," he snapped. "She's crazy!"

As the man with the grey hoodie stomped away, my mum sank to the ground, sobbing uncontrollably.

I sat with her and made up my mind. I was going to do it tonight.

CHAPTER 4

CHICKEN

I waited until I heard Dad come in from the shed. He made himself a cup of tea, watched TV for a while, then went to bed.

Ten minutes later, I slipped everything I needed into an empty laundry bag and crept downstairs.

It had taken us hours to get home again. By the time we got back to the main road, the police had towed Mum's car away. We had to go down to the station and give a statement. I explained as calmly as I could that she'd thought she'd spotted her missing son, and that was the only reason she had abandoned her vehicle that way.

Thankfully, one of the officers on duty had been on the team investigating Stephen's disappearance all those months ago. She had a word with a few of her bosses, and Mum was let off, with a warning not to do it again.

Back at home, she went straight up to Stephen's room and lay on his bed for an hour, before giving me some money for the chip shop and heading to her own room for the night.

I nipped down the road and picked up fish and chips for me and Dad, but he didn't come up from the shed to eat his. I gave it to Tonto in the end. Not the ideal dinner for a snake, but it gave some poor defenceless mouse an extra 24 hours, I suppose.

I'd found my phone in the gutter near where we had left the car. The screen was cracked, but it still worked. I quietly closed the kitchen door behind me, then sent Angel a text:

I'm ready.

A moment later, my damaged phone vibrated, the light from the shattered screen lighting up the kitchen. I read Angel's reply:

b there in 2 mins.

Grabbing Dad's keys from the hook near the fridge, I slipped out of the back door and hurried down the path to his shed.

I was still setting things out when Angel arrived.

"Are you sure about this?" she whispered.

I nodded, lighting some of the candles I'd brought with me so that we could see what we were doing. I didn't want to put the main light on and alert anyone to our presence. The flickering flames cast dancing shadows of my Dad's model ships around the walls.

"It was horrible," I sighed, lighting the final candle. "She was certain it was Stephen. I've never seen her that upset before – not even when he first disappeared. It's not about me any more. I'm doing this for her."

"And you think we can bring him back by doing this?"

I shrugged. "Nothing's certain, according to the book. But, at the very least, we should find out if he's still alive somewhere."

"And if he's not?"

I didn't reply.

"How are you going to explain that to your Mum?"

"I… I can't," I admitted. "I'd just have to let her carry on hoping. Now, give me a hand before I change my mind!"

We laid a rug on the hard wooden floor and began to unpack more items from my laundry bag.

I heard Angel catch her breath as she pulled out the book. "Is this it?"

"Yep," I said. "The best the Wiccan forum could provide – or, at least, the best I could afford. I spent all my holiday money on that thing."

Angel flicked through the pages. "The spell parts aren't in English," she pointed out.

I snatched the book from her hands. "Well, of course they're not!" I scoffed. "Anyone would be able to understand them then, wouldn't they? They're in… I dunno… magic language."

Angel stared at me. "Magic language?"

"I don't know, do I?" I hissed. "I'm just going to say it out loud and hope it makes sense. Now, I'll read out the list of things we need, and you make sure we've got them."

"OK," she said, sliding the laundry bag onto her lap. "Go for it."

"Fourteen candles," I said.

Angel counted the flames around the room.

"…Twelve, thirteen, fourteen. Check!"

"One white cloth…"

Angel pushed her hand into the bag and retrieved a cloth. "It's a tea towel."

I shrugged. "It's white, so it'll have to do. Next – one chicken…"

"Eurgh!" cried Angel. She tipped the bag up and a frozen supermarket chicken tumbled out. "Isn't it supposed to be alive?"

"Where am I going to get a live chicken at this time of night?"

"I dunno," said Angel, prodding at the solid, uncooked bird. "Will this one work?"

"We'll find out, won't we?" I said. "Now, last of all, we need a live animal to act as our witch's familiar. I've brought Tonto for that."

Angel peered down into the laundry bag. "He's not in here," she said.

"What? Then where is he?"

We spent the next fifteen minutes searching the shed for my pet snake, eventually finding him curled up asleep on the deck of my dad's model of the Titanic. I placed him on the floor next to the chicken.

"Is he alright?" Angel asked. "He's not moving as much as usual."

"I think it's the fish and chips I gave him earlier," I said. "I don't think it agreed with him. Maybe there was too much ketchup."

We both looked down at Tonto as he curled himself tightly around the chicken. Then he burped.

CHAPTER 5

OWL

By the time we'd got everything in place, it was almost midnight.

I raised the knife I'd borrowed from the kitchen above the rapidly defrosting chicken. "Ready?" I asked.

Angel nodded. "What do you have to do first?"

I glanced down at the book, squinting to read the tiny writing in the candlelight. "We have to slaughter the chicken as a gift to the demons."

"Off you go, then," said Angel. "Slaughter the already dead chicken."

Trying to ignore her sarcastic tone, I brought the knife down and stabbed the frozen chicken through its cellophane wrapping. The knife stood upright and wobbled a bit.

"Is it dead yet?" asked Angel.

I sighed. "You're not helping, you know!"

Angel pulled an innocent face. I went back to the book and read the first part of the spell out loud.

"Rakh nas tavla spla takh nakhu!"

Angel blinked. "Are you OK?" she whispered.

I nodded, concentrating on the book. "Why?"

"You sound like our cat trying to hack up a fur ball."

I glared up at her. "You don't have to stay if you don't want to, you know!"

"You're kidding!" chuckled Angel. "I wouldn't miss this for the world! What's next?"

"Next we have to introduce our witch's familiar…"

Cautiously, Angel reached out and lifted Tonto up by his tail. Ordinarily, this would be his cue to wrap himself around your arm and give you a hug. But that didn't happen this time. Thanks to the fish and chips I'd given him earlier, he simply waved his head in the air a few times – then he threw up all down Angel's top.

She squealed as a combination of battered cod and day-old mouse guts slopped down her front. Throwing Tonto at me, she jumped up, knocking into Dad's workbench and toppling half a dozen of the candles.

"Angel!" I shouted. "Be careful!"

The first thing to catch fire was Dad's half-finished model of the QE2 cruise liner.

I don't know what kind of wood he made these models from, but it was quick to burn.

I grabbed the white tea towel from the floor and tried to batter out the flames, but they were spreading fast. Within seconds, I was surrounded by spitting towers of fire.

The shed quickly filled up with smoke and I began to cough, unable to clear my throat properly. Maybe if I sat down for a moment I might be able to breathe better…

"Poppy!" squealed Angel.

"It's Raven!" I spluttered.

"Whatever – just get out of there!"

I felt a hand grab my sleeve and pull me out through the shed door. Instantly, the cool night air washed over me and I bent double, coughing like mad.

"Tonto!" I wheezed when I was able to catch my breath.

Angel jiggled the still unwell but, thankfully, still alive snake now draped around her neck. "I wasn't able to save the chicken, though," she said as she pulled her mobile from her pocket and dialled 999.

While Angel gave the fire brigade my address, I heard a flapping sound and turned to watch a large owl land in the branches of the tree at the end of the garden. It studied me with curious eyes, flecked with the orange reflection of the blazing shed. Then it looked past me, up towards the house.

I turned and followed its gaze to find my Dad standing just outside the back door, silently watching as his precious models – the ones he'd been making ever since Stephen disappeared – went up in smoke.

"Dad— " I began, taking a step towards him. But he went back inside the house without a word. I'd done it again!

A few seconds later, my mum came charging down the garden, alerted to the problem by the sound of approaching sirens. She scooped me and Angel up in her arms and made us promise over and over again that we weren't hurt.

Once the blaze was out, Angel gave the attending police officers details of what had happened. Not that we'd been trying to use witchcraft, of course – just that we'd met up in secret and used candles to light up our night-time den.

Mum led the fire crew up to the house for a cup of tea before they left, and I poked around the sodden remains of what was left of the shed, hoping to see my book of spells somehow still intact.

Of course, it was nowhere to be seen. It had burned up completely in the fire. So I set off to follow the others back indoors – and that's when someone grabbed me and pulled me into the bushes.

CHAPTER 6

RAVEN

I tried to scream for help, but a hand clamped over my mouth and kept me silent.

"You really are a fool, aren't you?" hissed a voice in my ear. "We've been doing magic around here for four hundred years and no one has suspected a thing. You make one ham-fisted attempt at a seeking spell and bring half the local law enforcement down on us!"

I twisted my head round to try to see who it was that was holding me. But all I could make out was a shadowy face, hidden by the hood of a cloak. Bright, owl-like eyes gazed out at me.

The figure holding me sighed and pulled her hood away, revealing herself.

I gasped. "Miss Cowl?" It was the deputy head at school who'd given me the lecture about the colour of my hair. "You're a witch?"

She pressed her palm against my mouth again. "Be quiet!" she warned.

I nodded and she removed her hand again. "How did you know how to attempt a seeking spell?"

"I bought a book on the internet," I told her.

Miss Cowl sighed. "I knew the web would cause trouble for us," she moaned. "Where's the book now?"

"It burned up in the fire."

"Well, that's one good thing…"

I pulled myself free of the witch's grip and spun around. "No, it's not!" I cried. "How can I find out where my brother is now? Mum and Dad deserve to know. If there's any chance I can help them I have to try."

Miss Cowl sighed. "OK," she said after a moment. "I haven't done anything like this in a very long time but, what if I were to find your brother for you?"

My eyes grew wide. "You'd do that for me? For my family?"

The witch nodded. "But I'd want something in return…"

I chuckled. "Like what? My soul?"

"Yes," said Miss Cowl.

There was a brief moment of silence.

"I'm sorry," I said, my throat suddenly dry. "For a minute there, I thought you said that you wanted my soul."

"I do," said the witch. "Well, not in the way you probably think. You'd still get to keep it, but I'd own it. You would become one of my coven of witches."

I blinked up at her. "I'd be a real witch?"

Miss Cowl smiled. "Would you like that, Raven?"

"I... I... Yes!" I cried, almost jumping up and down with excitement. "You mean, I'd get to learn to do spells and everything?"

"One thing at a time," said Miss Cowl. "The newest member of a witch coven acts as a servant throughout their training period. Are you prepared to wait on us hand and foot in our cottage in the woods?"

"You mean I'd have to leave home and move in?" I asked.

"Perhaps not straight away," Miss Cowl replied. "After all, it would not help your parents if I were to find one of their children, then whisk the other away on the same night."

"Exactly!"

"No, you may live at home until you leave school," said Miss Cowl. "But you would still be at our beck and call twenty-four hours a day…"

"So long as you find Stephen, I don't care," I said.

Miss Cowl lifted a wisp of my pink hair and examined it. "You'd have to change your appearance to fit in with the rest of my girls," she said.

I nodded my agreement. "No problem."

"Then the deal is done," said the witch. "Now, allow me a moment to concentrate…"

She closed her eyes and took a deep breath. For a moment, I imagined I heard the heavy flutter of owls' wings all round me, then the sound was gone.

Miss Cowl opened her eyes. "He lives," she said.

I suddenly felt light-headed, and was forced to cling on to her cloak to stop myself from fainting. "Stephen is alive?"

"And in very good health," smiled the witch. "In fact, he is just a little over 19 miles away from here – well within the range of a teleportation spell. Would you like me to bring him home?"

"You can do that?"

"I would do anything for a member of my coven," Miss Cowl smiled. "Now, Raven – watch the door to your house…"

I'd just managed to focus my eyes on the back door when there was a shudder in the atmosphere, as though I was suddenly looking at the house through a blast of hot air. I blinked against the effect and – there was my brother, standing in our back garden!

"St— " I tried to call his name, but Miss Cowl quickly had her hand over my mouth again. "Let him decide…" she hissed.

I watched as Stephen looked around, realising where he suddenly was. For one horrible moment, I thought he was going to turn and run away. But he didn't. Instead, he pushed the back door open and stepped inside.

I only heard one voice before Miss Cowl spirited us away. It was Dad, shouting: "Stephen!"

CHAPTER 7

RAT

We appeared at the doorway to a cottage, somewhere deep in the woods, and my brain suddenly made a connection.

"You're the group that has been in all the papers!" I said. "The ones dancing around at night."

"The very same," said Miss Cowl. "Thankfully, this cottage is protected by a sightless spell – no one will ever find us here. Shall we?"

The witch pushed open the small wooden door and stepped inside. I paused for a second to try to take everything in. From this moment on, I was a witch! I would have to work hard while I trained – but I would train. I would learn how to do real magic!

"Hurry, Raven!" called Miss Cowl. "Come and meet your sisters…"

Fighting the urge to grin, I pushed open the cottage door and stepped inside.

Then I froze.

I don't know exactly what I was expecting – perhaps a large cauldron in the middle of the room, jars of potions stacked onto shelves, rats running freely across the floor, and a gaggle of young hags cackling together in the corner.

But not this…

The entire cottage was decorated with posters of pop stars. Twinkling fairy lights covered every available surface, and the heavy stench of expensive, celebrity perfume hung in the air.

"Like, what's she doing here?" cried a familiar voice.

I stared at the group of girls standing before me, all their eyes fixed on me instead of their phones for once.

"She's our newest member," said Miss Cowl. "I recruited her."

Tiffany Langer glared. "But she, like, broke my nose, yeah!"

"And I repaired it," Miss Cowl pointed out. "Now, put your phones away for once and help Raven feel more at home…"

Tiffany clicked her chewing gum and grinned. "Whatever, Miss Cowl!"

The most popular girl in school held out a hand, and one of her cronies slapped a large tub of make-up into her palm. It was labelled 'Orange Sunrise'.

She took a step towards me. "Time for, like, a make-over, innit?"

Oh no!

THE END